Taylor,
I have heard lots
of good things about
I thought you might enjoy
this cut story. Great
message for all women.

Hugs,
Jim DeFronzo
Dec. 2015

A MODERN-DAY FAIRY TALE
for GROWN-UP GIRLS

THE Enchanted TRUTH

KYM PETRIE

 GREENLEAF BOOK GROUP PRESS

Published by Greenleaf Book Group Press
Austin, Texas
www.gbgpress.com

Distributed by Greenleaf Book Group LLC

For ordering information or special discounts for bulk purchases, please contact Greenleaf Book Group LLC at PO Box 91869, Austin, TX 78709, 512.891.6100.

Design and composition by Greenleaf Book Group LLC
Cover design by Greenleaf Book Group LLC

Publisher's Cataloging-In-Publication Data
(Prepared by The Donohue Group, Inc.)
Petrie, Kym.
  The enchanted truth : a modern-day fairy tale for grown-up girls / Kym Petrie. -- 1st ed.
  p. ; cm.

  ISBN: 978-1-60832-368-5

  1. Princesses--Fiction. 2. Man-woman relationships--Fiction. 3. Coming of age--Fiction. 4. Love stories, American. 5. Fairy tales. I. Title.
PS3616.E87 E63 2012
813/.6

Part of the Tree Neutral® program, which offsets the number of trees consumed in the production and printing of this book by taking proactive steps, such as planting trees in direct proportion to the number of trees used: www.treeneutral.com

Printed in the United States of America on acid-free paper

12 13 14 15 16 17   10 9 8 7 6 5 4 3 2 1
First Edition

TreeNeutral®

The way to read a fairy tale is to throw yourself in.

—W. H. Auden, poet (1907–73)

Introduction

This isn't any ordinary "Once upon a time . . ." I mean, haven't we all had enough of the garden-variety beautiful princess, horde of elves, glass slipper kind of fable? Let me tell you: A girl can't always count on Prince Charming to wake her from a hundred years of heavy sleep. This is a story you can sink your teeth into. A magical fairy tale . . . the story of the enchanted truth.

CHaPTer one

Once upon a time in a kingdom much like yours and mine, there lived a beautiful Princess. A sad, silly Princess whose heart had just been stomped on by the man she thought was her Prince Charming. And so, like all of us have, she threw herself into an angry, tearful stupor, whining about her misfortunes, screaming about the injustice of love, hating all those she had ever dated or wanted to date. She cried. She moaned. She ate heaps of junk food. She wished her perfect partner would soon drop out of the sky so she could get on with her life.

One sweet, dewy spring morning, Her Royal Highness awoke to find a sea of pink ruffles perched on her windowsill. The pampered imperial jumped out of bed and threw her arms around the rosy winged woman.

"This is it; she's come to answer my wish," thought the Princess, who was nearly insane with excitement. "My Fairy Godmother will fix everything now."

Before the fairy could say a word, the anxious aristocrat asked the round, wee woman, "How does this work again? Do I get three wishes, or do you just want to go straight to the 'poof' part and bring Prince Charming here ASAP?"

The magical visitor cast a wondering glance.

"*Wait!*" the Princess yelled, her heart pounding wildly now. "I bet you'll bring me to the royal pond, won't you?" She stuck her head through the open window to get a better view. "That's it, isn't it? Oh, this is my favorite fairy tale! I bet he's just been sitting on his lily pad waiting for me for weeks. Let's go, then; let's get to it. Introduce me to my Frog Prince!"

The frantic girl raced to her bedroom door still dressed in her nightgown.

"Oh, dear," whispered the pastel pixie loudly, "perhaps you should take a minute to collect yourself."

She floated toward the puzzled noble. "First things first,

my dear child. I am, indeed, your Fairy Godmother, but today I came *only* to introduce myself and to bring you a small gift."

The ingenue looked distraught. "Is it my Frog Prince?" she asked hopefully.

The glowing guest shrugged her pink-ruffled shoulders and shook her head no. A small squeaky whine escaped the Princess.

"I've brought you a gift, my dear," the bedazzled tutor said again, patting the maiden's arm softly. "A magical gift."

The fairy held out a dainty hand, and in her palm was a small leather lifeless frog. The frog wasn't real.

The novice regal rolled her eyes and let out a huge guffaw.

"You've got to be *kidding* me," she growled as she leaned in to poke the toy with her finger.

"Indeed I am not," sighed the fairy as she carefully placed the shriveled souvenir in the fair damsel's hands. The Princess looked at the frog carefully, surveying his wrinkled skin and distorted face.

"Why wouldn't you grant my wish?" asked the Princess. "What good will *this* do me?"

"Take your time, my dear," offered the zealous zenith. "We both know this is not the first time your heart has fallen prey to a badly behaved beau. You aren't ready for your Prince just yet . . . you have much to think about first."

The fledgling monarch set the small leather frog on her

bedside table and took a long look at him. His eyes sparkled. His mouth hung open in a crooked grin.

"What is it you want in your Prince?" asked the luminous visitor. "Take the time to think about what you desire in a partner, my dear, or you will continue to make the same mistakes choosing your mate."

"I *do* know what I want in a partner!" snapped the Princess. "But I am cursed! The men I've dated fool me; they trick me intentionally. My suitors present themselves as honorable men, but they turn out to be someone other than that completely. Each time I think I am falling for Mister Right, and then what happens? *Bam!* The guy turns out to be a fraud, a swindling scoundrel, or a dishonest, disparaging jerk!"

"Darling girl," cooed her bubbly benefactor, "those you choose to date are exactly who they have always been. In the past, you have chosen to ignore that truth. We have to date many a toad before we find our Prince. The frog I have given you will help you be true to yourself. He will help you be real and sure in your choices."

The Princess picked up her ornamental amphibian and flicked at one of his floppy legs. She turned him on his side and took a look at his sand-filled belly. An empty pocket was sewn into his underside. She looked at her Fairy Godmother again, who was floating toward the window, making ready to leave.

"The pocket is a place where you can keep your decisions."

The fairy said in a sweet, soothing voice. "It's in our quiet, simple moments of reflection and solitude that we find truth. Write down everything you desire your partner to be. Place your desires into the pocket and leave them there."

"That's *it*? Then what? How will that make a difference in my choices? How will that make me more ready?" The Princess folded her arms across her chest and glared at the sweet-faced winged woman.

"Think of him as your dating conscience, my dear," her charmed adviser said with a smile. "A reference point to keep your dating decisions in check. Sometimes a young maiden's libido can get the better of her common sense." She floated out the window in a pale pink cloud of lace and ruffles.

The Princess drop-kicked the tiny stuffed frog across her room.

CHapter two

That frog lay sunny-side up on the Princess's floor for days, but time had not stood still in the Kingdom. It was quite apparent that the Princess had discarded her mini-mentor's advice in the same manner she had tossed the congenial curiosity aside on the carpet. The lovely young lady had begun to date a very handsome young man from the castle next door.

"He's gorgeous," she bragged to her royal court, "and so funny. He has a great future in orchards and a brand-new convertible carriage, top of the line. My mother loves him. We had *so* much fun again last night."

The drawing room was loud with infectious giggles and the rustling of gowns. The pretentious nobles were far too busy sharing gossip to pay attention to the obvious disdain the servants had for the fair-haired regal's latest crush. No one took notice as one of her handmaidens shot the others a questioning look. The Prince next door was such a player, but far be it for her to say anything.

That night, while the Princess was waiting in the parlor for the Prince to pick her up for their third date (he was only forty-five minutes late . . . surely there was a good reason), the Butler entered the room and delivered a small brown envelope addressed to the Princess. Thinking it was a love note from her handsome neighbor, the Princess tore it open excitedly. On the front of the card was a picture of an ugly brown toad.

"He is *toadily not* for you" read the card. The Princess sat in stunned silence. She dropped the card on the Butler's tray and made her way up to her bedroom and out onto her balcony for a breath of much-needed fresh air.

"Who would send me such a note?" she fumed. She stomped her feet and had begun to throw a small tantrum when she noticed the Prince's carriage pull up next door. She watched as the footman opened the carriage door and helped a beautiful woman out of the gleaming vehicle. The Princess felt her chest tighten as the Prince, too, climbed out from the sparkling, steed-pulled chariot and wrapped his arm around the dishy damsel's waist, nuzzling her neck and stroking her back.

"That bastard," grumbled the Princess. "How could I have been so stupid?!" She slammed the door to the balcony behind her and threw herself onto her bed. Heaving sobs echoed through the castle as she cried the night away.

Chapter Three

A Fairy Godmother keeps a busy schedule of appointments with each of her needy, bereft maidens, and the one assigned to our Princess was no different. Our effervescent sidekick popped in and out to see the Princess as often as she could and always kept her fingers crossed that the lovely young thing would start to learn her heart's lessons and move on into her own life with what meager support the Fairy Godmother could give. She tried to be as subtle as she could on her visits but was wondering what it would take for this naive Princess to get with the program.

"Geez," the fairy thought to herself, "what is it with these girls nowadays? Do they really think that everything will just fall into their lap? When will they learn that happiness isn't a gift that comes to rescue you on horseback . . . it's a light you have to reach for *inside*?"

The Fairy Godmother surveyed the Princess's bedroom. It was littered with the remains of chocolate bars, potato chips, and ice cream containers. She swept cheesy crumbs off the bed and sat softly beside the grieving girl. The Princess's face was puffy and streaked with mascara.

"What is *wrong* with me?" the Princess wailed.

"My dear, you have to learn how to be true to yourself. Did you take the time to write down what you desire in a Prince as I reminded you to? If you had, would this one have lived up to the expectations you had listed? I think not. Your tender heart was not meant to be cared for by a man who is always on the prowl. Haven't you always said that you want an honest, respectful partner who finds *you* to be the most interesting?"

The Fairy Godmother clucked away, gently scolding the young Princess. "Surely it is more important to have a caring prince than one who drives a hot new carriage. You deserve a partner whose *character* lives up to your expectations."

For a while longer, the Fairy Godmother consoled the

Princess before making her way out the window and on to the rest of her day. She looked back at the defeated girl lying rumpled in her bed and heaved a heavy sigh.

CHAPTER FOUR

Many more days passed, yet the small leather frog remained crumpled in a corner of the Princess's room. One morning after waking with the dawn, the fair maiden lay still in her bed, contemplating the fate of her love life for what seemed like hours. When the sun started to cast long shadows throughout her snack-scattered yet sumptuous suite, she finally slid out of bed and crossed the room to her dressing table. Still rumpled, drowsy, and dressed in her nightclothes, she searched through the drawers and pulled out a pen and paper.

"One day my Prince will come," the Princess wrote, "and when he does, he will be . . ." She began to list all of the qualities she desired in a partner, sometimes hurriedly scribbling down thought after thought, but more often than not, sitting still, thinking quietly about what was important to her before adding to the list. When she finished, there were many pages on the dressing table, each one filled with her deepest thoughts and desires. She folded the papers neatly and knelt down to pick up her teeny stuffed frog. She placed the notes into his belly pocket and set him down gently on her night table. Frog looked at her directly now, full and proud—her sand- and secret-filled sentinel.

CHAPTER FIVE

Despite the exercise of writing down her thoughts, as her Fairy Godmother had advised, our redolent regal still had not made the acquaintance of her Knight in Shining Armor. Little had changed, and as much as she tried, the Princess found it difficult to keep her mind from circling back to how incredibly lonely she was. The lanky lass had rarely left the castle in weeks, and it was starting to become obvious that a gallant hero was not on the immediate horizon. She knew she had to make the effort to change her daily landscape so she took matters into her own hands.

Her Highness swallowed her pride, threw on her big girl bustle, and stepped bravely into the world of single chickdom.

She sent notes to friends, arranged divine dinners, and stretched the limits of her once small and pretentious social circle. She dragged girlfriends to museums and the theater, took salsa lessons . . . even went spelunking. Sure, a few available men were around, but the Princess was quick to take note of any "royal flags" in their conversations or behaviors— clues that showed a potential suitor's true colors.

She made a conscious effort to stop whining about her single status and start doing the sorts of things she would normally have expected to do with a prospective prince. In fact, she began to set aside some time each week to take herself out on a date.

Each morning she greeted her stuffed frog with a wink and a nod, and each night she gazed over at him as she settled into bed.

There were many times the content of her notes came to mind, and often, after meeting an enthusiastic suitor, she realized there were additions to be made. Her wobbly bauble had grown considerably: his weathered skin now stretched to its limit as he held an ever-expanding slate of the Princess's considerations.

One damp and foggy evening after watching a particularly curious foreign film, the Princess and her gaggle of girlfriends made their way to a fabulous new wine bar. There she found herself in the company of an exceptionally gallant member of the King's Round Table. The pair sidestepped the crowd and moved to a quiet spot in the back, where he steadied his dark and brooding gaze on her and leaned in to share a bit about himself. What started out as a scintillating tale of courage and strength soon turned tedious and yawn worthy.

The minutes ticked by like hours, and the Princess desperately tried to signal a friend to save her from the situation. The hunky Knight may have freed the small village from the likes of that dastardly dragon, but Her Royal Highness had spent the evening as his conversation hostage.

Upon arrival back at the castle, she ran up the stairs two at a time, shot across her bed to reach the frog, and promptly added *humble* to the list.

On another occasion, whilst pulling on her life jacket and helmet for an adventure-filled day of white-water kayaking with the gang, the Princess was introduced to a wealthy explorer who had recently arrived home to a hero's welcome after leading the Queen's Navy to a new and savage land.

"So pleased to make your acquaintance," he said as he smiled broadly and bowed with a grand sweep of his arm. His voice was low and confident, his hands quick and adept as he pulled her closer to buckle her gear and offer suggestions pertaining to paddle handling and balance. He gripped, he tightened, he explored—that's for sure. His wandering hands were far more interested in the curve of her bustline than her safety during the trip. Before she even made it halfway across the dock to her kayak, she made a mental note to add to her checklist the word *respectful*.

A change in the Princess was noticeable, and the Queen was not amused by her unladylike antics. One afternoon following a lecture at the university, the pensive imperial took a leisurely stroll back home. This gave her the much-welcomed chance to walk through the sweet fresh grass and gardens along the path from the auditorium. The fountain danced and gurgled, the birds sang, the pond shimmered under a cloudless blue sky.

Her Mother met her at the door, and they shared small talk as they made their way through the hall and up the staircase into the regal daughter's room. The Princess leaned back in her chair, finding within it a quiet corner. The Queen sat tall on a sumptuously covered sofa, looking over the finery that had been laid out for the Princess to change into. She spied her daughter's curious comrade still propped on the bedside table, its belly taut and mouth agape.

When the Queen suggested that the Princess was becoming too independent and high-spirited, the fair maiden jousted, dauntless, "Mother, I am *not* going to sit around waiting for a man while my life goes by . . ."

The matriarch sighed and lowered her voice to a sweet

whisper. "Darling, you have had some interesting suitors vying for your attention. What about the men who have been courting you?"

The spirited scion leaped out of her chair and began to change into her evening clothes, waving her petticoats in utter frustration.

"I know those men aren't for me—" The novice royal had barely finished her sentence when the Monarch raised her voice in surprise.

"How could you so quickly?" she interrupted. "You've hardly had time to get to know them."

"*Mother*," the Princess sighed, sliding into her yellow satin heels and straightening the neckline of her gown. "Of course I've had the time. It isn't so hard to look beyond their gleaming new carriages or manicured good looks."

The two women walked back down the stairs and into the cavernous foyer surrounded by the soft amber warmth of sunset. The low, long chimes of the palace clock signaled the hour, and the meddling monarchical mother slid her arm around her daughter's shoulder.

"I am starting to wonder," said the Queen, "if that ugly toy frog hasn't put some sort of spell on you. It seems you have lost interest in searching for your true Prince Charming since it's been on your night table."

The Princess smiled and squeezed her mother's hand quickly before stepping out of the castle and into the carriage for a night out with the girls.

CHaPTeR SIX

As in all good fairy tales, time tripped by quickly. Months passed and seasons changed. Late one evening while the autumn breeze filled her bedroom and the stars brightened the crisp, cool night air, the Princess found herself staring at the oddly angelic toy amphibian perched by her bed, eyes ever sparkling and grinning his crooked leather smile.

She lifted him up and gave him a kiss. Yes, *she kissed her frog.*

Had her Fairy Godmother been right? The Princess hadn't been ready to find her Prince so many months before. Back then she thought her life would be perfect once her Knight in Shining Armor came along. Wasn't that what her mother had always taught her? Wasn't that how all of her storybooks ended?

She knew now that happily-ever-after wouldn't simply meet her at the end of the aisle.

The Princess removed the papers from her curious comrade's pocket. It had been months since she'd read through her list. She held the "journal of expectations" up to the window for light and smoothed the folds of the paper.

Her eyes raced through each line. The list went on for six pages.

A breeze whirled gently through the room and the Princess looked up to see her Fairy Godmother sitting on the windowsill. The Princess stopped reading and sat up in bed; her ethereal envoy was always such a welcome sight. The tiny woman's magic wand glistened in the moonlight.

"Fairy Godmother, may I ask you a question?" said the Princess.

The powerful pixie leaned down toward the bed and cooed in her sweet voice, "Ask away . . ."

"Why do you always carry that wand? Is it part of the

Fairy Godmother uniform? Mandatory wings, ruffles, wand? I've never seen you use it."

The fairy looked down at the wispy golden scepter in her hand. "I don't know why we still carry it nowadays," she said thoughtfully. "Fairy tales would have you believe that a Fairy Godmother can grant a wish with the wave of her hand, but that was never really the case. Sure, I can conjure up a few pretty gowns and occasionally a carriage or two, but those in my profession weave their spells to grant insight and inspiration. We help remind people that the magic they seek has been within them all along. It's the magic of inner spirit that makes one's dreams come true."

The stewardly sprite looked at her watch and jumped up with a start.

"My dear girl," she exclaimed, "I must hurry. I have a rather distraught young maiden to attend to. She's had a wicked time with her fiancé lately—no surprise, really. Some of the other Fairy Godmothers and I have been biding our time waiting for the other glass slipper to fall, so to speak. I really need to run." She blew a kiss and made her exit.

The Princess sighed and snuggled into her pillow. That poor maiden, she thought; it was so obvious who it was. The Princess knew just what that girl needed: a pollywog pal and some time to discover herself. She made a mental note to give her a call and invite her out with the girls.

She turned her attention to the secret jottings still lying on the bed and propped herself up to continue her reading. When she reached the end of her thoughtful list, she folded the pages carefully and stuffed them back into her homely hero's pocket. His front legs flopped over the side of her night table. He looked at her with wise, knowing eyes.

It all made sense now. For years she had struggled with self-confidence and doubt, but now the young royal truly believed she was worthy of a partner who lived up to her expectations. More than that, she knew she had *become* the type of person her heart had yearned for; it was within her all the time. Courageous, tenacious, loyal, honest, funny, and forthright. No wonder she had lost the desire to find a partner who would complete her. She *was* complete.

The Princess sighed once more and leaned back against her pillows. She got it. She knew the enchanted truth . . .

"I am my own Frog Prince," she said aloud. The stars were brighter, the air fresher.

"I am my *own* Frog Prince!" She smiled contentedly. And for now, that was enough.

THE END?
NO WAY. THIS IS ONLY THE BEGINNING.

ACKNOWLEDGMENTS

When I wrote this story more than a decade ago, I had no idea where it would lead me. I now know this to be true: Women are powerful enough to determine the outcome of our own fairy tales, but it won't fall into our laps. There is simply nothing more satisfying than watching someone find their true Prince Charming because, ladies, it's not a PRINCESS we find when we look deep inside ourselves . . . it's a hero on horseback.

Couldn't imagine that any of this would have been

possible if it weren't for the women who pulled me kicking and screaming through some of the most horrifyingly sad moments of my life. To Andrea Carmichael, Ellen Nightingale, Marnie Stone, Nadia Sartor, who held my hand, kicked my ass, and taught me to drink vodka martinis. You saved my life. Lori Lehtimaki, Kim Briel, Jill Zago, for the healing power of laughter. Jill Armstrong Braido, whose passion and determination impacted my teenage years and have simply never left me. Adele Lynagh, Heather Hough, Melinda Lehman, Lana Hockey, Susan Beam, Holly DiGiovine, who showed me there is nothing more beautiful than a fearless, brilliant woman.

To the original, unique, and amazing Carole Hunt and my sweet sister Andrea, for helping me believe I was strong enough to take anything on. Robbin Phillips, Tami Fremlin, Bobbi Johnson, who find the best in every person they meet and whose underlying strength and conviction can move mountains.

To Mary Biebel and Sheila Cheek, whose adventurous hearts and exquisite minds brought the enchanted truth full circle into its new life. You welcomed me home.

To Alice, who taught me that being joyful, powerful, and sexy is a decision. Eighty-six looks great on you!

To Rick Mitchell, Eric Brown, Jim Boyd—love you madly.

To Pat Staub, Taryn Scher, Stephen Williams, Hobbs Allison, Linda O'Doughda, Sheila Parr, Natalie Navar, and the Greenleaf Team, for bringing my dreams into hardcover reality.

To the fabulous Miss Shae. How things have changed. Writing your story helped me change mine.

To my boys, Cole and Spencer, the LOVE of my life. Now that I've done this you have to do something you think is truly impossible.

To Ron, for the challenge, the love, the laughter, and being all that I whispered to my secret list (and so very much more). You are my best friend.

To Laurie, for the flowers in my hair and the dreams in my heart. To Mom—I will remember for you. To my superhero father, who taught me to fish, play hockey, throw a good punch, follow my heart, and follow through. Hey Dad, look at this! Pretty good for a girl, eh?

ABOUT THE AUTHOR

Kym Petrie wrote *The Enchanted Truth* for a friend who was caught up in a desperate search for Prince Charming. The tale had an unexpected impact; it inspired Kym to take a closer look at the choices she herself was making.

Canadian born and bred, Kym is now living happily ever after with her family in South Carolina. This is her first book ...